# USBORNE FIRST READING
## Level Four

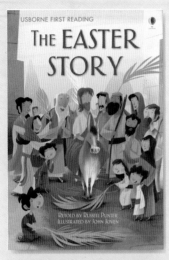

USBORNE FIRST READING

# THE EASTER STORY

RETOLD BY RUSSELL PUNTER
ILLUSTRATED BY JOHN JOVEN

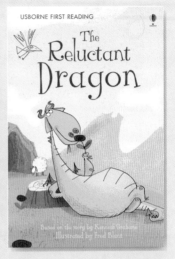

USBORNE FIRST READING

# The Reluctant Dragon

Based on the story by Kenneth Grahame
Illustrated by Fred Blunt

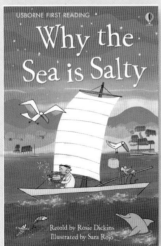

USBORNE FIRST READING

# Why the Sea is Salty

Retold by Rosie Dickins
Illustrated by Sara Rojo

USBORNE FIRST READING

# Thumbelina

Retold by
Susanna Davidson
Illustrated by Petra Brown

# Clever Jack and the Giants

## Susanna Davidson

## Illustrated by Leo Broadley

Reading consultant: Alison Kelly

Jack sat by his window.
He had bread.

He had jam.

He was happy.

Yum yum.

...came a noisy fat fly.

Buzz

Buzz

Buzz

"Shoo!" cried Jack. "Shoo! Shoo! Shoo!"

5

But more flies came.

"Take this, you pests!"
cried Jack.

He swatted the flies and
they fell to the ground.

"Seven dead!"

"I must tell the whole world about this!" said Jack.

He cut out a banner and then began to sew.

When he had finished, the
banner said:

Seven with one blow!

Jack put on his banner.

He took some cheese to eat.

He picked up his pet bird.

Then he went out into
the world.

He hadn't gone far when...

He met a giant.

"Ha!" laughed the giant, peering at the banner.

"Seven with one blow? I don't believe it."

"It's true!" said Jack,
proudly.

"How about a test?" said the
giant. "Let's see how strong
you are."

The giant picked up a stone.
He squeezed and squeezed,
until...

...water dripped out.

"Easy-peasy," scoffed Jack.
He took out his lump of
cheese.

"Watch this!" Jack said.

He squeezed and squeezed
until that dripped too.

"Humph," snorted the giant. "I bet you can't throw as far as me."

He picked up a rock and hurled it into the air.

It flew up so high, it was just a dot in the sky.

"Easy-peasy!" said Jack.
"I can throw things so high,
they never come back."

22

He took out his pet bird
and threw it in the air.

The bird flew
up, up, up into
the sky.

23

"It's not coming back!"
gasped the giant.

Wow!

"I hate being beaten,"
the giant grumbled.

"But this little man is really strong. I need some help!"

"Come and spend the night
in my cave," said the giant.
"You can meet my friends."

It was dark when they
reached the giants' cave.

Jack went straight to bed.
But in the night, he heard
whispers.

So he jumped from the bed,
crept behind a rock and
waited...

At midnight,
the giants came.

They smashed the bed to tiny
pieces.

Thwack!

Crack!

"Ha! Ha! Ha!" laughed the
giants. "That's the last we'll
hear of him."

The giants fled in terror.

Jack marched to the next village.

"I've killed seven with one blow," he boasted. "And I've scared off ten giants."

"Really?" said the villagers.
"Then we need
your help."

"Two huge giants live
in the woods over there.
They trample our houses."

"They eat our cows. Can you get rid of them?"

He found the giants fast
asleep in the woods.

I know what
to do!

Jack picked up some stones
and climbed a tree.

The giants began to fight.
They uprooted trees...

...and smashed them over each other's heads.

Take that!

Then they both fell to the ground, dead.

After that, Jack went up and down the land.

"I've killed seven with one blow," he boasted.

Jack became famous.
He became a hero.

All because some flies liked
his jam.

## About the story

*Clever Jack and the Giants* is based on a German fairy tale, *The Brave Little Tailor.* It was retold by the brothers Jacob and Wilhelm Grimm.

Designed by Sam Whibley
Series designer: Russell Punter
Series editor: Lesley Sims

First published in 2015 by Usborne Publishing Ltd.,
Usborne House, 83-85 Saffron Hill, London EC1N 8RT, England.
www.usborne.com Copyright © 2015 Usborne Publishing Ltd.

# USBORNE FIRST READING
## Level Four

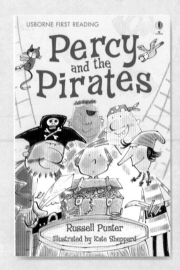

USBORNE FIRST READING

**Percy and the Pirates**

Russell Punter

Illustrated by Kate Sheppard

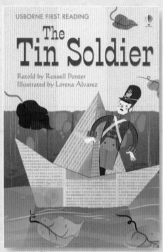

USBORNE FIRST READING

**The Tin Soldier**

Retold by Russell Punter
Illustrated by Lorena Alvarez

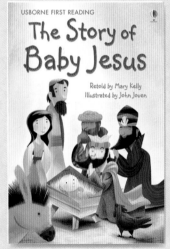

USBORNE FIRST READING

**The Story of Baby Jesus**

Retold by Mary Kelly
Illustrated by John Joven

USBORNE FIRST READING

**The Owl and the Pussy Cat**

Edward Lear
Illustrated by Victoria Ball